This book belongs to:

. . . .

. . . .

Reading Together

This story is written in a special way so that a child and an adult can 'take turns' in reading the text.

The left hand side is for the adult to read.

"Rapunzel, Rapunzel, let down your hair," called the Prince.

The next day the prince went to the tower.
"Rapunzel, Rapunzel, let down your hair," called the prince.
Rapunzel let down her hair.
The prince climbed up it.
Rapunzel was surprised to see the Prince.
Soon they were friends.

The right hand side has a simpl[e] sentence (taken from the story) which the child reads

Firstly, it is always helpful to read the whole book to your child, stopping to talk about the pictures. Explain that you are going to read it again but this time the child can join in.

Read the left hand page and when you come to the sentence which is repeated on the other page run your finger under this. Your child then tries to read the same sentence opposite.

Searching for the child's sentence in the adult version is a useful activity. Your child will have a real sense of achievement when all the sentences on the right hand page can be read. Giving lots of praise is very important.

Enjoy the story together.

I Can Read...

Rapunzel

Once upon a time there was a poor man.
His wife was having a baby.
She was very sick.
She needed some lettuce to make her better.
The lettuce only grew in the garden of
a witch.

The lettuce only grew in the garden of a witch.

The poor man stole the lettuce.
The witch caught the poor man!
The witch said the poor man could keep
the lettuce.
"But you must give me your baby,"
said the witch.
The poor man did not know what else to
do, so he said yes.

The witch caught the poor man!

Soon the baby was born.
The poor man and his wife called their
baby Rapunzel. They had to give her to the
witch because they had made a promise
that they would. Rapunzel grew up.
She had long golden hair.

The poor man and his wife
called their baby Rapunzel.

The witch hid Rapunzel in a tall tower.
There was no door in the tower.
There was only a window.
Every day the witch visited Rapunzel.
"Rapunzel, Rapunzel, let down your hair,"
called the witch.
Rapunzel let her hair down out of
the window.
The witch climbed up Rapunzel's hair.

Every day the witch visited Rapunzel.

One day a brave Prince was riding in
the forest.

He saw the witch climb up Rapunzel's hair.

One day a brave Prince was
riding in the forest.

The next day the prince went to the tower.
"Rapunzel, Rapunzel, let down your hair,"
called the prince.
Rapunzel let down her hair.
The prince climbed up it.
Rapunzel was surprised to see the Prince.
Soon they were friends.

"Rapunzel, Rapunzel, let down your hair," called the Prince.

The Prince visited Rapunzel every day.
One day Rapunzel told the witch about
him. She did not mean to but she did.
The witch was angry.
She cut Rapunzel's hair off.
She sent Rapunzel away.

The Prince visited Rapunzel every day.

The next day the Prince went to the tower.
"Rapunzel, Rapunzel, let down your hair,"
called the Prince.
The witch let down Rapunzel's hair.
The Prince climbed up.
He was very surprised.
Rapunzel was not there.
The witch was there.

Rapunzel was not there.

The witch threw the Prince out of
the window.
The Prince landed in some thorns.
The thorns got in the Prince's eyes.
He could not see.
The Prince walked into the forest.
"Help me!" cried the Prince.

The witch threw the Prince out of
the window.

Rapunzel heard the Prince.
She was very sad and started to cry.
Rapunzel's tears washed the thorns out
of the Prince's eyes. He could see again!
Rapunzel and the Prince fell in love.
They lived happily ever after.
The witch ran away and never troubled
anyone again.

Rapunzel and the Prince fell in love.

Key Words

Can you read these words and find them in the book?

tower

cottage

Prince

witch

Rapunzel

Mix and Match

Draw a line from the pictures to the correct word to match them up.

Family

tower

Rapunzel

Prince

witch

bird

Prince

bird

fell in love

hide

lettuce

Tell your own Story

Can you make up a different story with the pictures and words below?

family

cottage

tower

witch

Questions and Answers

Now that you've read the story can you answer these questions?

a. What did the poor man steal from the witch's garden?

b. Who pushed the Prince out of the tower window?

c. Who got thorns in their eyes?

a. A lettuce   b. The witch   c. The Prince